For Jasper, River and Fabrizio

First published 2017 by Walker Books Ltd
87 Vauxhall Walk, London SE11 5HJ

This edition published 2019

2 4 6 8 10 9 7 5 3 1

© 2017 Christopher Silas Neal

The right of Christopher Silas Neal to be identified as the
author and illustrator of this work has been asserted by him
in accordance with the Copyright, Designs and Patents Act 1988

Printed in China

This book has been typeset in Sabon

British Library Cataloguing in Publication Data:
a catalogue record for this book is available from the British Library

ISBN 978-1-4063-8421-5

www.walker.co.uk

This Walker book belongs to:

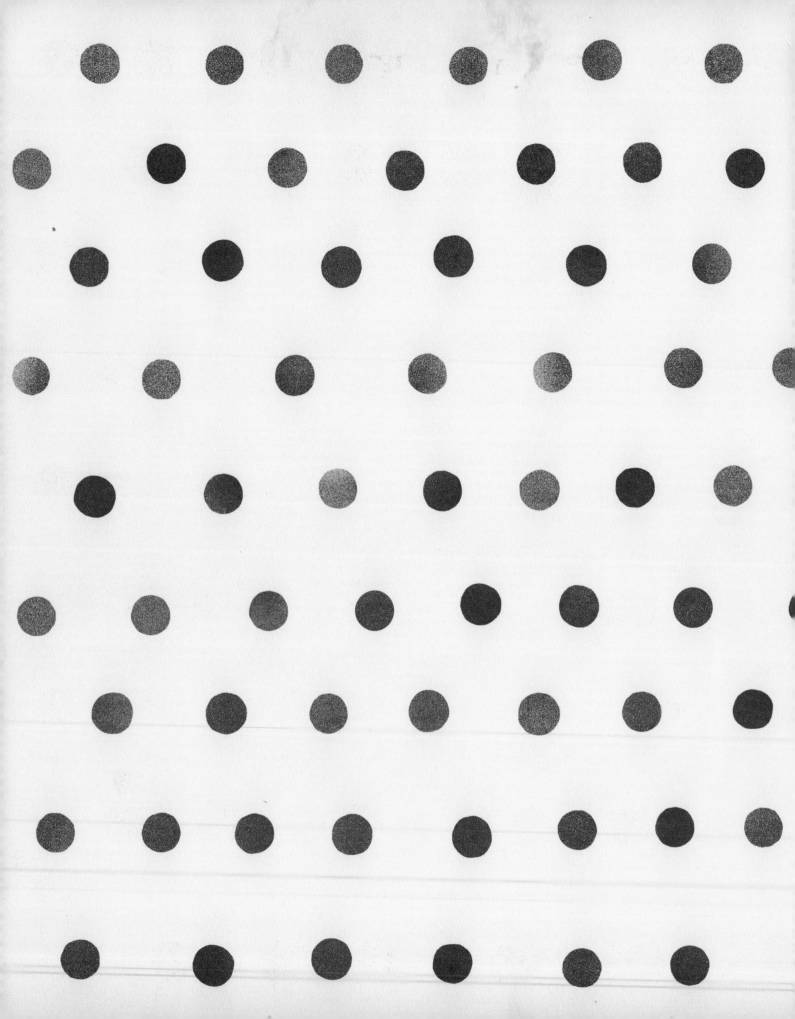

I WON'T EAT THAT

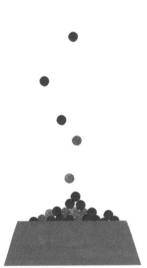

Christopher Silas Neal

WALKER BOOKS
AND SUBSIDIARIES
LONDON · BOSTON · SYDNEY · AUCKLAND

Dogs eat dog food.
Fish eat fish food.

But I'm a cat,
and I will NOT eat cat food.

It's dry and dull and not very yummy.
Yuck.

But if I don't eat cat food,
what will I eat?

"Hello, Tortoise.

I'm hungry and searching
for something yummy to eat.

What does a tortoise eat?"

"Worms, of course.
But I must warn you, they wiggle."

"Eww. No, thank you."

"Hello, Fox.

I'm hungry and searching
for something yummy to eat that
doesn't wiggle.

What does a fox eat?"

"Rabbits," replied Fox, as he pounced
on a furry, long-eared critter.
"But I must warn you, they bounce."

"Whoa."

"Hello, Chimp.

I'm hungry and searching
for something yummy to eat that
doesn't wiggle
or bounce.

What does a chimp eat?"

"Ants," replied Chimp. "We use sticks to get them out of trees
But I must warn you, they bite."

"Yikes! I won't eat that!"

"Lion, please help.

I'm hungry and searching
for something yummy to eat that
doesn't wiggle,
bounce,
or bite.

What does a lion eat?"

"Zebras!" roared Lion, as he sprang after his striped prey.
"But I must warn you—"

"Never mind. There is NO WAY
I'm eating one of those."

"Excuse me, Elephant.

I'm so very hungry and searching
for something yummy to eat that
doesn't wiggle,
bounce,
or bite
and that isn't too big.

What does an elephant eat?"

"Lots and lots of grass.
But I must warn you, it's a little dry."

"Ugh. That's even MORE BORING
than cat food."

"Hey, Whale! Up here!

I'm really hungry and searching
for something yummy to eat that
doesn't wiggle,
bounce,
or bite
and that isn't too big,
too dry,
or too boring.

What does a whale eat?"

"My food is perfect," sang Whale.
"It's none of those things, and it certainly isn't boring.
In fact, my food glows in the dark.

But I must warn you, it's hard to pronounce.
It's called bioluminescent phytoplankton."

Phyto-what? Whale's food is too weird.
Isn't there anything yummy for me to eat?

"Hi, Cat," squeaked Mouse.
"I'm hungry and searching for something yummy to eat.
What does a cat eat?"

"Hmm …
I think I've just figured it out.
But I must warn you…"

Christopher Silas Neal

is the illustrator of a number of books for children and is the author-illustrator of *Everyone...* He also teaches illustration at the Pratt Institute in New York and is a regular contributor to *The New York Times*. Born in Texas and raised in Florida and Colorado, Christopher now lives in Brooklyn, New York. Find him online at csneal.com, on Twitter as @csneal and on Instagram as @csilasneal.

978-1-4063-7327-1

"The message of self-acceptance and community
is heartfelt and reassuring"
The New York Times

Available from all good booksellers

www.walker.co.uk